BUILT FOR SPEED

STOCK CAR

Holly Cefrey

HIGH
interest
books

Children's Press
A Division of Grolier Publishing
New York / London / Hong Kong / Sydney
Danbury, Connecticut

Book Design: Christopher Logan
Contributing Editor: Jeri Cipriano

Photo Credits: Cover © Allsport/Andy Lyons; pp. 4, 6, 9, 11, 13 © The Image
Bank; p. 15 © AP Photo Archive; p. 17 © Allsport; pp. 18, 20 Allsport/Robert
LaBerge; p. 22 © AP Photo Archive/Pryor; p. 25 © Allsport/Donald Miralle; p.
26 © AP Photo Archive/Kathy Willens; p. 29 © Ap Photo Archive/Peter A.
Harris; pp. 30, 40 © AP Photo Archive/Dave Martin; p. 32, © AP Photo
Archive/Daytona Beach News-Journal, Sam Cranston; p. 35 © AP Photo
Archive/Steve Helber; p. 36 © AP Photo Archive/The Albuquerque Tribune,
Kevin W. Weinstein; p. 38 © AP Photo Archive/Chris O'Meara;

Visit Children's Press on the Internet at:
http://publishing.grolier.com

Library of Congress Cataloging-in-Publication Data

Cefrey, Holly.
  Stock car / by Holly Cefrey.
    p. cm. — (Built for Speed)
  Includes bibliographical references and index.
  ISBN 0-516-23164-2 (lib. bdg.) — ISBN 0-516-23267-3 (pbk.)
  1. Stock car racing —Juvenile literature. [1.Stock car racing.] I.
Title. II. Built for speed

GV1029.9.S74 C39 2000
796.72'0973—dc21

                                                        00-063898

CONTENTS

INTRODUCTION

A loud voice echoes over the racetrack: "Drivers, start your engines!" You flip on your car's ignition switch. The engine roars to life. Your hands shake on the steering wheel from the powerful engine vibrations. All around you, other racecars are lined up just inches away. The go-ahead is sounded to move toward the track. Shifting the car into first gear, you head down pit road. You drive side-by-side with other racers around the track. As you come down the front stretch, you shift into fourth gear. You're watching for the green flag. Within seconds, the starter drops the green. The race is on!

At the start of a NASCAR race, all drivers shift into high gear. The roar of the engines can be deafening.

Welcome to the exciting and fast-paced world of stock car racing. Perhaps you have dreamed of becoming a stock car racer. Maybe you would like to be one of the crew members who builds racecars and keeps them running at top speeds. Or perhaps you just want to sit back and watch the action from the comfort of your living room. Any way you want to enjoy the sport, stock car racing is a thrilling ride!

In the United States, stock car racing started in the Southeast during the 1920s. Today's stock car racing is very different from its early days. Why did the drivers start racing in the first place? They were trying to outrun the law!

BOOTLEGGING — THE BEGINNING

From 1920 to 1933 it was illegal to make, sell, or possess alcoholic beverages in the United States. The 18th Amendment to the U.S. Constitution forbid it. This period of time was known as Prohibition. Even though alcohol was illegal, many people still wanted it. So some people broke the law by making and selling their own whiskey. This illegal alcohol was called *moonshine*. Moonshiners had to be

This is what stock car racing looked like in the 1930s.

Standard cars like these were the kind bootleggers used.

careful and very clever to avoid getting caught by police officers or county sheriffs.

Delivering moonshine became known as bootlegging. Bootleggers put the moonshine in their cars and carried it to their customers. Because they often had to outrun law officers, bootleggers worked on their car engines to make them run faster. They also removed extra seats from the cars to make them lighter and to allow room for more moonshine.

Bootleggers were proud of their cars. They started challenging each other to races to see whose car was the fastest. These races took place mostly on dirt roads. Later, farmers carved oval dirt tracks in fields. These farmers (and sometimes the moonshiners themselves) figured people would want to come and see the races. They were right. Local people began to watch the races and to cheer on their favorite drivers. When Prohibition ended in 1933, bootlegging also ended. But stock car racing had just begun.

ORGANIZING THE RACES

Racetrack owners realized that they could make money from the races. They began to charge admission prices to the races. Track owners promoted races by offering cash prizes to the winners. Some promoters, however, left town without paying the winners. At that time, there were no organizations to protect racers from bad promoters. One racer, named William France, set out to protect racers. He also wanted to get more people excited about the sport of stock car racing. France helped make stock car racing the thrilling sport that we know today.

William France

In 1934, William "Bill" France traveled through Daytona, Florida. France was a mechanic who had already raced cars on dirt tracks. One day he watched a speed show on the beach. France became so excited about the Daytona racing area that he moved there. In 1936, Daytona city officials decided to hold auto races on the beach. They built a track that was 3.2 miles (5.2 km) long. Half of the track was on the beach. The other half was on a highway that ran next to the beach. Bill France drove in the first race and finished in fifth place.

In 1938, France became a race promoter. During the next ten years he promoted a series of successful races. These races ran on tracks throughout the South. He named the series the National Championship Stock Car Circuit. On December 14, 1947, France held a meeting for racers. He presented the idea of a national organization for stock car racers. The

By 1951, stock cars such as this one were used in NASCAR races.

organization would promote racing and bring to it order and respect. Bill France was elected president of this new organization. It was named the National Association for Stock Car Automobile Racing, or NASCAR.

NASCAR

The first NASCAR race was held in Daytona, Florida, in February, 1948. Even though Bill France wanted drivers to race new, modern cars, NASCAR allowed older cars into the race. By 1949, though, France's wish of using only new cars came true. They were called stock cars because they were regular, or stock, cars that people could buy at a car dealership. France believed that people would want to watch races featuring cars that they could buy themselves.

The drivers could not modify anything on their cars except the engines. They modified the engines to make their cars run faster.

Driver Bobby Sall is thrown from his car during a test run at a Daytona Beach Stock Car race in 1936. Early stock car drivers didn't have the safety precautions today's drivers have.

Drivers would drive their cars to the track, tape their racing number on the car, and then race. If they didn't crash during the race, they drove their cars home.

NASCAR SAFETY RULES

Years passed and stock cars became faster and faster. These higher speeds increased the risk of crashes and injuries. Stock cars of the early 1950s had no safety equipment. Drivers simply used ropes to keep themselves tied to their seats. Then in 1953, seat belts became required equipment. By the 1960s, stock cars were reaching speeds of 150 miles (241 km) per hour. NASCAR began making rules that would lower the risk of death and injuries in crashes. Drivers had to wear helmets. The driver's cockpit had to have a roll cage to protect the driver. Fuel tanks had to be leakproof. These and other safety rules began to save lives on the racing circuit.

Here is a look at stock car racing in the 1960s.

NASCAR SERIES

NASCAR races are divided into several series. The top NASCAR series are the Winston Cup, the Busch Grand National, and the Craftsman Truck series. Each series holds races during the racing season throughout the United States. Points are awarded to each driver who finishes a race. Finishing first, second, or third earns more points than finishing in the last three spots. The points are recorded for every race. At the end of the season, the drivers that have the most points win awards.

Fun Fact

In 1949, driver Red Byron won one of the first NASCAR races. It was held on the beach and road course at Daytona Beach, Florida. Byron won $2,000. Fifty-one years later, driver Dale Jarrett won the Daytona 500. Jarrett earned more than $2 million!

Different racecars are used for different series. Busch Grand National cars look similar to Winston Cup cars, only they are lighter and less powerful cars. Craftsman series racecars are modified pickup trucks. They are much lighter than the other two series cars, and they handle differently on the track.

Pickup trucks are featured in the NASCAR Craftsman truck series.

Under
THE HOOD

Today's stock cars are completely different from the original stock cars. For one thing, modern stock cars are no longer "stock." In other words, you can't buy one from your local car dealer. In fact, modern stock cars are specially built by racing teams. These teams spend many hours making the cars as fast and as safe as possible. NASCAR tests each car to make sure that it meets the same standards. NASCAR wants each team to have an equal chance of winning.

THE STOCK CAR

A stock car has three main parts: the body, the chassis, and the engine. Building a racecar

Stock cars may use the shells of regular cars, but they are very different under the hood.

The roll cage and the harness help protect the driver from serious harm.

takes two weeks and costs more than $100,000. The building of the car begins with the chassis (frame). Then the body is then shaped and added to the chassis. The engine is the last part to be added.

The Chassis

The chassis is a steel structure beneath the body. It holds together all the parts of a car.

The lower part of the chassis holds the brakes, wheels, and parts that steer the car. The engine and transmission are held in place by the chassis, as well.

The main part of the chassis is called the frame. The frame is made of strong, tubular steel. The tubular steel is measured, cut, bent, and welded to form the steel structure. The frame weighs about 600 pounds (272 kg).

One of the most important parts of the chassis—and one that is not found in regular cars—is the roll cage. A roll cage is a cage made of steel tubing that surrounds the driver's seat. If a car crashes, the roll cage helps protect the driver from injuries. You may have seen a serious crash during a stock car race. Sometimes the car flips over and over again, breaking into hundreds of small pieces. The driver often walks away from the crash with only minor injuries. Drivers survive bad wrecks because of roll cages and harnesses.

Richard Petty's car crashed into the wall during the February 14, 1988, Daytona 500. Thanks to his car's safety gear, he was able to walk away from the accident.

The Body

The body of a stock car is the outer metal casing. A racing team can choose from one of the body styles created by American carmakers and approved by NASCAR. Even with different body styles, stock cars share certain similarities.

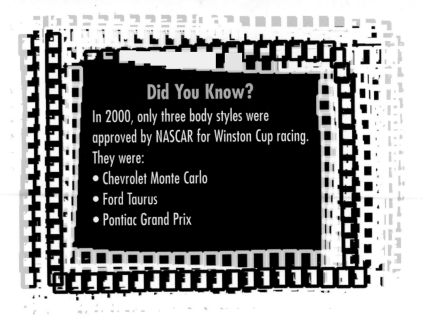

Did You Know?

In 2000, only three body styles were approved by NASCAR for Winston Cup racing. They were:

- Chevrolet Monte Carlo
- Ford Taurus
- Pontiac Grand Prix

For example, all stock cars have only one seat—for the driver. The car doors are welded shut so they cannot open or close. And there is no window on the driver's side. The space where the window would be is where the driver climbs into the car. During races, a netting covers the open space. The netting stops any flying objects from entering the car.

Instead of glass, windshields are made of a special plastic that resists breaking. Plastic windshields won't break into sharp pieces during a crash. Stock cars don't have headlights, either. Races that are held at night are run under bright racetrack lights.

Today's stock cars use only a few parts taken directly from an automobile manufacturer. The roof, hood, and trunk lid are stock parts. Those parts on a Ford Taurus stock car, for example, will look the same as those parts on a Ford Taurus that you might see in an automobile showroom.

The Engine

Teams can build, buy, or rent stock car engines. To keep cars at safe speeds, NASCAR limits the horsepower of racers' engines. The higher the horsepower, the faster a car can go. NASCAR makes drivers use restrictor plates to keep the engines from going too fast. Racing teams try to adjust the engine so that it has the highest possible horsepower even with the restrictor plate. Winston Cup stock car engines can go to 700 horsepower. Even with restrictor plates, NASCAR racecars reach speeds of more than 200 miles (322 km) per hour.

Stock car motors are tuned to perfection so they can go very fast.

DRIVERS,
Start your Engines!

Racecar drivers get most of the credit for winning a race. Winning any NASCAR race, however, takes a team effort. No racecar driver works alone. Without the mechanics and crew working behind the scenes, no driver would leave the pit—let alone win a race!

DRIVERS

Driving stock cars is a dangerous business. Racecar driving demands skill and dedication. Getting the chance to race alongside more than thirty other cars takes a lot of practice and preparation.

Bill Elliott leads the field in his pole position at the start of the 1987 Daytona 500.

Driving Safety

Racing at high speeds requires special safety equipment. Drivers wear special uniforms to protect themselves. Everything they wear—right down to their underwear—is designed to resist fire. Drivers also wear helmets to avoid head injuries. Inside the car, drivers are strapped to their seats with five-point safety harnesses. This kind of harness holds a driver in place across the legs, shoulders, and chest.

Driving Style and Racing Lines

Every stock car driver has a different racing style. Some drivers race smoothly and steadily in a tight pattern. Other drivers race wildly and at full speed. Driving style is important. It can affect how much gas is used and how the car and tires hold up during the race. A driver should have an idea of what makes the car handle best on each track. Most drivers will try to find and hold a racing line. The racing line is the fastest way around a track.

The pit crew must work together as a team to help drivers win races.

Driving Rules

NASCAR has safety rules for racecar drivers. These rules protect all drivers on the track. Drivers must have some racing experience and be in good physical shape. Drivers must be able to stay mentally focused during a race that lasts hundreds of laps. Even a split-second break in focus can result in a crash. Any crash can cause serious injuries.

Before stock car drivers can race in a Winston Cup race, they need a competitor's license. To qualify for a license, drivers need to

Drivers rely on their pit crews to refuel the cars and change the tires in the shortest time possible.

be at least sixteen years old and must pass a physical exam. NASCAR then examines the driver's racing experience or makes the person take a driving test. Only when drivers pass all tests will they be allowed to race.

PIT CREWS

Racing at speeds of 200 miles (322 km) per hour is very tough on cars. Stock cars need to stop several times during a race for gas and fresh tires. Engines may need to be worked on, also. The pit crew does all of this work. Pit crew members need to be very good at what they do. They also need to work fast.

Pit Stops

While racing, drivers service their cars during pit stops. Pit areas are located off the race-track, along pit road. A small concrete wall separates the pit crew from pit road. A pit crew is made up of twelve members. Seven are allowed over the concrete wall and onto pit road. The other five must stay behind the wall. These five may hand tools back and forth to the other members. Each pit crew member has one job. Jobs include changing tires, refueling, and cleaning windows.

During a race, every second counts. If the car spends too long in the pits, valuable racing time is lost. Even the fastest drivers can lose a race because of a long pit stop. That's why top-notch pit crews are fast and sharp. They help drivers win races.

The
RACING LIFE

Winning races is why stock car drivers race. The fans of stock car racing want to see their favorite drivers win. Watching a race can be exciting, entertaining, and educational. By paying close attention to winning racing styles, many beginning racers become better racers.

BEING A RACING TEAM MEMBER

What's it like to be a member of a racing team? It can be fun and exciting. But it also demands a lot of hard work and can be very tiring. Team members work long hours and travel almost year-round. They must be comfortable with living on the road and staying in hotels. Team members often face

Shawna Robinson answers reporters' questions after finishing second in the ARCA FirstPlus Financial at Daytona International Speedway held in Daytona Beach, Florida, on February 7, 1999.

Fun Fact

Volunteering to help a racecar driver can be very rewarding—and a lot of fun! The auto body shop students at the Bucks County Technical School in Pennsylvania know this out firsthand. For several years now, these students have painted the cars driven by stock car racer Andy Belmont. The students created the blue, yellow, and white design of Belmont's cars. They also have painted the helmets that he wears. Whenever Andy Belmont wins a race, these students surely feel like winners, too!

many challenges in turning an average racecar into a winning car. Many crew members say that the chance to meet these challenges is why they joined a racing team. Being a part of a winning team outweighs the long hours and nonstop travel.

Successful drivers are always in demand for public appearances. You might have seen your favorite stock car driver at an auto show. Sometimes drivers sponsor community

Pit crews line up along pit row before the 1996 Hardee's 250 stock car race at the Richmond International Raceway.

volunteer organizations. When drivers aren't racing or practicing, they usually work with the public somehow.

Working with the public means that drivers must be people-friendly. They often chat with fans and sign autographs. Sponsors arrange the appearances so that their products get

Every Saturday night fans flock to Duke City Raceway in Albuquerque, New Mexico. Here, the Street Stock Division holds races on a dirt track.

publicity, as well. These appearances take place all over the United States, so drivers must travel for public appearances as well for races.

EDUCATION AND JOBS

There is always room for new members in the world of stock car racing. Racers who don't do well with one racing team often leave and join another team. Crew members also may switch teams. Many racers and crew members started their careers by visiting a local track. Getting to know a local driver or racing team is a good way to find out all about racing. Volunteering to help a crew is another way to learn about racing. You may want to be a driver, but helping the crew will give you valuable information about teamwork.

Another way to learn about racing is to attend a racing school. Racing schools give you the opportunity to drive and understand stock cars. This experience can help you decide if racing is for you. Some schools offer training for other jobs in racing besides that of driver. Many of these schools offer degrees relating to the world of racing. A graduate of these schools can start in a better position or with a better salary.

STARTING SMALL

Many drivers and crews come to the NASCAR series after racing at lower levels. Racing go-karts, sprint cars, or motorcycles is a good way to get started. This kind of racing is much

On February 6, 1999, Jeff Gordon took the lead position for the Daytona 500 with a qualifying speed of 195.067 miles per hour. Here he is posing next to the billboard showing his time.

less expensive than stock car racing. To learn more about go-kart, sprint car, or motorcycle racing, visit a track in your area. Another way to find out about races is to visit a local shop that sells go-karts or cycles.

Starting on a smaller level gives drivers valuable racing experience. They learn about engines, racing strategies, and teamwork. Drivers experience different racing styles without worrying about sponsors or winning. They are able to develop their skills at their own pace. There are racing schools for go-kart, sprint car, and motorcycle racing, as well as for other kinds of racing. No matter what your level of interest—as a spectator, crew member, or future driver—the world of racing offers many opportunites for learning.

Jeff Gordon

One famous driver who started out small was Jeff Gordon. Born in Vallejo, California, in 1971, Gordon began his racing career when he was only five years old! At that age, he raced quarter midgets. Then he moved on to go-karts, which he raced until he was thirteen. He won several championships with both types of vehicles. On his sixteenth birthday, Gordon received his racecar driver's license for the United States Auto Club (USAC) circuit. This made him the youngest driver in USAC history. As an adult, Gordon has become a

Jeff Gordon gets a kiss from his fiancée after winning the NASCAR Brickyard 400 in August 1994, at the Indianapolis Motor Speedway.

skillful and popular NASCAR driver. In 1991, he was voted Rookie of the Year in the Busch Grand National series. In 1993, he earned Rookie of the Year honors in the Winston Cup series. The following year, he won his first Brickyard 400 in Indianapolis, Indiana. Jeff Gordon has continued his winning ways. He was the Winston Cup champion in 1995, 1997, and 1998.

FACT SHEET
Winston Cup Stock Car

Engine: 358 cubic inch V8, 700 horsepower
Transmission: four-speed manual
Body: Monte Carlo, Taurus, Grand Prix
Height: 51 inches (129 cm)
Weight: 3,400 pounds (1,542 kg)
Wheel base: 110 inches (279 cm)
Fuel: 22 gallons (.083 kl) of 104 octane 76 racing gasoline
Speed: 180 miles per hour (290 km/h) or more

NEW WORDS

bootlegging Delivering moonshine, or illegal alcohol

chassis The metal structure underneath the body of a car

horsepower The power level of an engine

moonshine Illegally-made whiskey

pit crew The team of people that services a racecar

pit crew member An individual member of the pit crew

pit road The road from the pits to the track where cars are started and serviced

pit stop A stop during a race when a racecar leaves the track to be serviced

restrictor plates Plates inside a carburetor that limit an engine's horsepower

NEW WORDS

roll cage A safety device made of steel
tubing that surrounds the driver's seat in a
stock car

sponsor A company that pays a racing team
to carry its name on their cars

stock Anything made direct from the
manufacturer

For Further READING

Huff, Richard. *The Making of a Race Car.*
Broomall, PA: Chelsea House Publishers, 1999.

Stewart, Mark. *Auto Racing: A History of Fast Cars and Fearless Drivers.* Danbury, CT: Franklin Watts Incorporated, 1999.

Sullivan, George. *Burnin' Rubber: Behind the Scenes in Stock Car Racing.* Brookfield, CT: The Millbrook Press, 2000.

RESOURCES

ORGANIZATIONS
United States

Automobile Racing Club of America (ARCA)
P.O. Box 5217
Toledo OH, 43611
(734) 847-6726

National Association for Stock Car Automobile Racing (NASCAR)
P.O. Box 2875
Daytona Beach, FL 32120
(904) 253-0611
Web site: *www.nascar.com*

RESOURCES

Canadian Association for Stock Car Auto Racing (CASCAR)

9763 Glendon Drive
Komoka, Ontario N0L 1R0
Phone: (519) 641-1214
Web site: *www.cascar.ca*

CASCAR Western Office

3650 19 Street
Bay 1 NE Calgary T2E 6V2
Alberta, Canada
Phone: (403) 250-3359

RESOURCES

Web sites

ESPN.com – Auto Racing

www.espn.go.com/auto

Find the current standings and racing results for your favorite drivers and races. This Web site contains information about all types of auto racing.

Racingschools.com

www.racingschools.com

This Web site provides a comprehensive list of racing schools for all types of racing.

SpeedFX

www.speedfx.com

Keep up-to-date with the latest news and information for all of the NASCAR series. This Web site also includes articles about NASCAR history and fun trivia questions.

INDEX

About the Author

Holly Cefrey is a freelance writer who comes from a racing family. Her brother was a World Karting Association and stock car racer; her father was a tech official and mechanic; and her mother was a scoring official.